Oh The Horror!

5 Horror Stories

REBECCA M. SENESE

OTHER BOOKS BY REBECCA M. SENESE

The Night Killers

The Color of Blood: The Chronicles of Richard Damon

Wreck the Halls: 5 Christmas Horror Stories

By Howl & Claw: 5 Werewolf Stories

With a Bite: 5 Vampire Tales

Bad Ends: 5 Horror Stories

In Dwarf Land and Cannibal Country

A Very Zombie Christmas

The Beginners Guide to the Recently Deceased

Needle Point

The In-Between Series
Book 1: A Reluctance of Blood
Book 2: A Remembrance of Flesh
Book 3: A Retribution of Soul

Oh The Horror!

5 Horror Stories

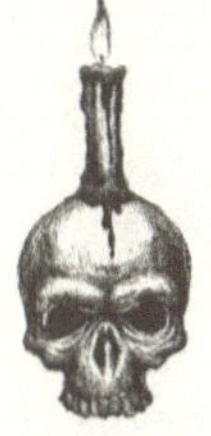

REBECCA M. SENESE

RFAR Publishing
Toronto, Canada

Published 2012 by RFAR Publishing
Toronto, Canada
http://www.RFARPublishing.com

Trade paper edition designed by Rebecca M. Senese
in InDesign CS5.5

Electronic editions designed by Rebecca M. Senese

Cover design 2026: Rebecca M. Senese
Images © Anke / CanStockPhoto.com
100er / DepositPhotos.com
S-E-R-G-O / DepositPhotos.com

ISBN: 978-1-927603-00-0

Publications Acknowledgement

"Here Comes the Rain." First published in *Storyteller*, 2007.

"In the Walls." First published in *Storyteller*, 2008.

"These Premises Protected By..." First published in *Storyteller*, 2007.

"Returning Home." First published in *The Vampire's Crypt*, 1998.

"Soul Hungry." First published in *On Spec*, 2006.

Oh The Horror!

5 Horror Stories

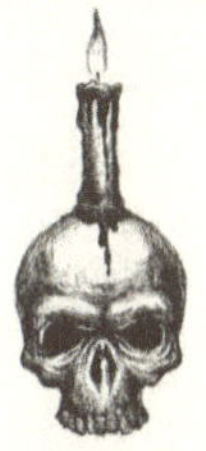

Table of Contents

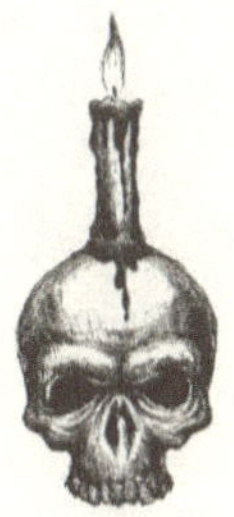

INTRODUCTION

Welcome to my first collection. I always have a slightly different view of things from other people. I notice something and it sends my mind off in a strange direction.

I guess that's what being a horror writer is all about.

I notice people running to get out of the rain and wondered, what would it be like if the rain really *was* out to get you. I hear about squirrels getting into the walls of someone's house and wonder, what if the squirrels conspired with the homeowner.

And so on.

I hope you enjoy these creepy tales, that they bring a smile to your face or a chill to your heart.

Until we meet again, our paths crossing on a dark road somewhere. Look, is there something behind you?

Rebecca M. Senese
October 2012

Here Comes The Rain

Eventually Paul noticed that whenever the sun was shining, Bertie made his appointments. When it rained or was heavily overcast, Bertie cancelled or simply didn't show. Probably inclement weather depressed him more, Paul thought, reminded Bertie of his inability to see through his own troubles. Might be something there to address.

On Tuesday morning, the sun blazed through a few wisps of cloud. When Paul opened his office door, Bertie perched on the edge of a waiting room chair, his narrow shoulders hunched. He sat in the same chair every time behind a pillar, hiding from the receptionist's view. Bertie raised his head at Paul's footsteps.

"Come in, Bertie."

Shoulders hunched, shrinking his height, he scurried past Paul and into the office. He sat at the far end of the sofa, pressed against the side as if by a brisk wind. Paul closed the door and crossed to his leather chair.

"How are you feeling today?" he asked.

Bertie pushed thick glasses up his nose. A delaying tactic. Paul waited, hands resting lightly on his lap. He didn't bother with a notepad during the session. Bertie seemed even more anxious. Paul made his notes afterward.

Bertie's slender shoulders quivered in an approximation of a shrug. "Okay, I guess."

"Did you have a look at the brochures I gave you?"

Bertie's long finger picked at a thread on the knee of his faded black pants. "Yes."

"What do you think?"

Panic flashed across Bertie's face. "I don't know. I don't think I could go."

"What did you think when you read them?"

"The Fun House." Bertie's words dipped to a whisper. "I remember the Fun House. Those mirrors. Like a million versions of me. And him."

"Bertie, that is very good. Just a few months ago, you couldn't even say the words 'Fun House'. Now you're looking at a carnival flyer. You're really taking control."

A shy smile tipped Bertie's lips. His shoulders dipped a little lower. He had always responded well to praise, Paul observed. Craving it and probably more so as a gawky child, making him the perfect target for a cruel predator. In the Fun House.

"I'd like you to keep the brochure for a while," Paul said. "Look at it everyday, even when it's upsetting. Spend at least half an hour looking at it."

Bertie swallowed. "Half an hour?"

Paul nodded. "I want you to get bored, sick of looking at it. I want you yawning at the thought."

Another smile twitched Bertie's lips.

"If you find you're already bored, you might

consider visiting a carnival," Paul said. "But that's entirely up to you."

The smile vanished. Bertie chewed his lower lip, pushed his glasses up his nose.

"If that's too much, just look at the brochure. We'll work our way up. Okay, Bertie?"

"Okay, Dr. Lansky."

"I'm leaving now Dr. Lansky, would you like me to lock the outer door?" The receptionist poked her head in.

Paul glanced at his watch. Already five-thirty. He'd finished with patients at four and was still writing up reports. "Yes, please, Sharon. See you Monday."

With a parting wave, she left, leaving him with the hum of fluorescent lights and the murmur of his hard drive.

Paul flipped through the remaining files. Another couple hours of work left. Damn paper work. He hated it and always left it to the last minute. Even during school, his professors had nagged him about updating charts. He'd thought once he was in practice and away from the insane mounds of homework, he'd settle into a routine of filling out the charts regularly. He even left time at the end of each day and what inevitably happened? He'd procrastinate to the end of the week and be struggling to convert his scribbled notes into coherent thoughts.

Finally by seven fifteen, he dumped the files into Sharon's in-tray for filing. The image of a cold beer filled his mind. The ringing phone caught his attention as he started to turn off the lights. His fingers hovered over the light switch. Who was that? He didn't often get emergency calls. The thought of a cold drink beckoned but he knew he couldn't enjoy it if he didn't answer the phone.

He returned to the desk. "Hello."

"Dr. Lansky, it's your answering service. I'm sorry to bother you but I have a patient on the line who won't hang up. Can you take him?"

Paul rubbed his forehead. "Yes, I'll take him."

"Just a moment." Several clinks sounded on the line, then another breathless voice whispered, "Dr. Lansky?"

"Yes, this is Dr. Lansky. Who is this?"

"Bertie." The voice faded out, then came back in a wild rush. "Help me, doctor, you've got to help me. I did like you told me and now it's coming. You gotta help. I wanna go home, please, help..."

"Slow down, Bertie," Paul said. "Where are you?"

"The carnival on highway ten." Bertie's voice cracked with desperation. "I did like you told me. I have to face my fears and now look what's happened." He trailed off with a whimper.

Paul took a deep breath to stop the sigh that threatened to come out. Any sign of exasperation would alienate Bertie. His problems were serious to him.

"Tell me what's happened," Paul said. "How did you get to the carnival?"

"I took a bus. Transferred north and walked from the last stop." A sob broke through. "I can't walk back now."

"It's okay, Bertie. Take some deep breaths and calm down. Remember how we practiced."

After a few moments, Bertie's ragged breathing slowed to a steady rhythm.

"That's better," Paul said. "Now I want you to call a cab and go home. On Monday, call Sharon and make an appointment to come in. I'll leave her a note to fit you in."

"No, I can't take a cab." Panic started to rise in Bertie's voice. "Please Dr. Lansky, I can't go out there. It'll get me. Please help."

So much for that cold beer. "Give me the address, Bertie."

He reached the carnival by eight thirty. It was set up in a field off highway ten. Paul could see the Ferris wheel through the sheets of rain. The lights sparked like a kaleidoscope because of the water.

Leaving the office, Paul had been surprised by the rain. He didn't remember hearing that in the forecast. He pulled the car off to the side where a hand painted sign said "Parking." A quick check in the back seat confirmed his suspicion. No umbrella. He turned his collar up and ducked out into the rain.

It was coming down in a torrential pour, as if the water was in a race to get to the ground. Three steps from the car, his hair was plastered to his head. He made it to the admissions booth where an elderly clerk demanded full price despite the weather.

Not bothering to argue, Paul paid and ran into the carnival, heading for the fun house and the direction of Bertie's phone booth. Halfway through the midway, he found a concession stand selling umbrellas and bought the largest one they had. It was brilliant yellow with large red dots, an impossibly cheerful umbrella against the cold, rainy night. Gratefully, he opened it and hurried toward the fun house, watching for Bertie. The carnival was deserted. Miserable carnies hunched underneath inadequate overhangings, not bothering to call out to him as he hurried by. He passed familiar games of chance and shooting galleries where he could have shot any number of things from balloons to metal bad guys. In front of the horse racing games, soggy stuffed animals hung dejected from the overhang. The carnie huddled in the back hadn't even bothered to try to rescue them.

He wanted to find Bertie and get out of here. The place was completely depressing. It would certainly do no good to Bertie's frame of mind.

A large, lopsided house came into view at the end of the midway. A peeling sign arched over the front door, spelling out FUN HOUSE in cartoon letters. Misshaped doors jutted out at odd angles. Crooked stairs led up the side before curving back toward the front where a pair of distorted mirrors reflecting only gray. Rain carpeted the entire house, and because it was so oddly shaped, it looked like it was melting. Not much of a fun house, Paul thought.

A moment later, he spotted the phone booth just to the left of the fun house. He hurried forward, his shoes squishing in the puddles. Condensation clouded the glass of the booth. As he drew near, the door opened a few inches and he saw Bertie peer out.

"Dr. Lansky," the man whimpered.

"I'm here, Bertie. It's all right."

"I did like you said. I tried but then the rain..." His voice broke off in a strangled cry.

"I understand. I'm very proud of you. This is a tremendous first step. Don't worry that you can't do everything all at once. You're trying and that's the important thing. It will get easier as you go along, Bertie." Paul lifted the umbrella to shade the doorframe to the booth. "Let's go now."

Color blanched out of Bertie's face. His head shook until his jowls jiggled. "I can't leave here. Not with the rain."

"It's all right now, Bertie. I've got an umbrella. My car is just in the parking lot. I'll drive you home."

More head shaking, so violent Paul feared the man's glasses would fly off. "I can't, no, I can't." He cowered back into the phone booth, letting the door slide shut. Paul caught the edge before it closed completely. He wedged his hip against it and pushed it open.

"What's wrong, Bertie? What are you afraid of?"

The umbrella in Paul's hand tipped as he

tried to lean in through the doorframe. Water trickled over the edge, dribbling down the glass door. Bertie gasped and pressed himself against the back of the booth.

"Don't come closer," he hissed.

Paul stopped and stepped back, using his foot to hold the door open. He tilted the umbrella, sending the water draining off behind him. "What is it, Bertie?" he said calmly.

Bertie's ragged breathing was his only reply. His glasses slipped down his nose, leaving his watery blue eyes bare and unfocussed. Sweat plastered his limp hair to his forehead in a strange reflection of Paul's own rain-soaked hair.

"Just tell me what is bothering you," Paul said.

Bertie mumbled something.

"What was that?" Paul asked.

"I can't go out," Bertie repeated, his voice barely above a whisper.

"Why can't you come out? Is it the Fun House?"

Bertie shook his head, the glasses sliding a little lower. Another head shake and they would fly off, Paul thought. Something in the image was vaguely comical, like a Three Stooges gag. Paul clenched his jaw. Stay focused, he told himself.

Bertie glanced around, as if checking if anyone was eavesdropping, then he leaned forward. Paul bent his head to catch Bertie's whispered secret.

"The rain."

"The rain?"

"Shh, it'll hear you." Bertie clenched the front of Paul's coat in one of his thin fingered hands.

"What will hear?"

"The rain." Another quick glance around and Bertie brought his head closer. "It listens and it waits. It's so patient. It waits for you to make a mistake so it can get you. It acts so innocent but all the time it's just waiting."

"What's it waiting for?" Paul said.

"For you to come out unprotected." Bertie's voice was stronger now, warming to his subject. He glanced around again, gripped Paul's coat tighter. "I've been too smart for it, bundle all up or don't go out at all but I slipped up tonight. Tonight it's gonna get me." His face paled as he spoke.

"Listen to me carefully, Bertie, the rain isn't going to get you." Paul kept his voice calm and quiet. He'd never heard of being afraid of the rain before; this was a new one. Obviously he was going to have to put Bertie on medication, maybe lithium, maybe something else. He'd have to do some reading up on it.

"It is," Bertie insisted. "You don't know."

"How does it get you?"

"It burns, it melts you away into nothing and all the while you feel it, scalding you." Bertie's voice rose to almost a shout, then he clamped his hand over his mouth, eyes bulging in panic in case the rain heard.

"Many people get wet in the rain," Paul said. "See my hair? It got wet before I bought this umbrella. It didn't scald or burn me, it only got me wet."

Bertie shifted inside the booth, his feet squishing in the damp earth. "It only goes after the ones that know. You didn't know before so it wouldn't get you."

Complete justification, Paul thought. He knew if he continued to argue, Bertie would come up with all kinds of justification for his position, no matter how unreasonable. He couldn't very well wait for the rain to stop before coaxing the man out of the booth, it looked like it was going to rain all night. He was going to have to do something drastic.

"Here, take the umbrella for a moment," Paul said.

Bertie blinked, then extended his hand shyly. His slender fingers grasped the handle tentatively, then with more strength.

"Got it?" Paul asked.

Bertie nodded.

"Good. Now watch."

Paul withdrew until he was completely out of the umbrella's protection. A strangled cry burst through Bertie's lips as the rain poured down onto Paul's shoulders. Paul felt the water dripping on his face, his hair getting slimy with wetness. His overcoat hung heavy from the water. He lifted his hands and extended them palm upward, cupping them. Water filled them. He stepped back under the umbrella.

"It's only water, Bertie," he said. "Look at it in

my hands. It doesn't burn. It doesn't melt. It just makes you wet."

One of Bertie's thin fingers extended toward Paul's palm. Paul watched the man's face as he touched the water. Uncertainty slowly replaced the panic like cream discoloring coffee.

"No burning," Paul said.

"No burning," Bertie whispered. He released the umbrella as Paul dropped his hands, letting the water run out, and then took the handle.

"This umbrella is big enough to cover both of us," Paul said. "My car is in the lot beside the front entrance. Only a few minutes walk away. You're doing so well with the Fun House, Bertie. You can easily defeat the rain. All you have to do is try."

Bertie fumbled with his glasses, pushing them hard against the bridge of his nose. The normal delaying tactic had become a decision-making trigger. Jaw clenched, Bertie slowly nodded.

Paul lifted the umbrella higher as he stepped back from the booth, all the while using one hand to hold the door open. Bertie took a cautious step forward, letting his foot down beside a puddle. His gaze darted down and he stopped, as if waiting to see if the puddle was going to attack him. Nothing happened. He took another step and then another, until he was completely out of the booth and standing hunched under the umbrella.

Paul had to stretch his arm to accommodate holding the umbrella high but he wouldn't ask Bertie to hold it. The man's nerves were stretched to the limit. His entire body trembled as he hunched inside his coat. His hands were white where they clenched the front closed.

"Just a few minutes' walk from here," Paul repeated in a soothing voice. "We'll take it slow. You set the pace."

Bertie's right foot slithered across the ground, barely half a step. Paul kept pace. Bertie paused, as if waiting to see what the rain would do. Then he took another step. Again the pause. One more step and pause. Each pause was successively shorter, each step a little wider. Paul wished him silent encouragement. Any distraction could cause Bertie to panic.

Despite the cool air, sweat glistened on

Bertie's forehead. A vein throbbed along his jaw with the effort of moving forward. They reached the midway and began moving past the games of chance. Even the carnies had disappeared, the games were packed up, presenting plain boards to the empty midway. Bertie slowed again as they came to several large puddles in succession. Paul reached his foot out and touched it with the toe of his shoe. No burning, no melting. He could feel Bertie watching him as he placed his weight on the foot. Water surrounded the leather. He imagined the frown on Beth's face and how long he'd have to spend cleaning the shoes. What the hell, maybe he'd pay someone to clean them if it got them out of here faster.

Bertie followed, taking small steps, balancing on his toes as if trying to let as little of himself touch the puddles as possible. A breeze ruffled the hair on his forehead until sweat caught the stray hairs and stuck to them. Around them, rain drummed a low accompaniment along the roofs of the stalls. Drips hitting the puddles offered a counterpoint.

A strong wind rose up, lifting the hair on

Bertie's forehead and even tugging at Paul's own wet hair. Paul pushed dripping strands back on his head. He didn't want water in his eyes now. The rain started coming down harder, and with the wind behind it, it began pushing toward them. The umbrella jerked in his hand. Paul tightened his grip. He angled the umbrella, trying to block as much wind as possible but it was picking up. God, what a hell of a storm.

Bertie stopped in front of a boarded up balloon toss game. They were almost to the front entrance, Paul could see the entrance booth, closed now.

"Almost there, Bertie," he said. "The car is in the parking lot just past the booth."

Bertie didn't respond, wasn't even looking at him. He stared forward, past the booth, toward the highway where the occasional eighteen wheel truck rumbled by, sending up a large spray like a whale. The wind flapped the collar of his coat.

"It knows. It's coming," he whispered. "It's been just fooling, but now it's coming."

"No, it isn't," Paul said firmly. "The car is just past the booth. Let's go." He shifted the umbrella and gripped Bertie's arm with his right hand. Pressure made the man take a half step forward.

"Let's go now, Bertie."

A sudden gust of wind flipped the umbrella inside out. Rain splashed into their faces. Bertie screamed, his hands flying up. Paul blinked away water. He tried to hold onto Bertie's arm but the other man pulled free.

"Bertie!"

"No, no!" Bertie cried. He ran, hands covering his face. Puddles tripped him up. He went down, landing on one knee before jumping up and racing off.

Paul dropped the umbrella and ran after him. Wisps of smoke rose from Bertie's coat along the collar and on his leg where he'd fallen. His feet slapped heavily in the mud. Paul pistoned his arms, running harder. He drew up beside Bertie, noticed how red Bertie's hands were from the cold.

"Bertie, wait," Paul shouted, but the other man didn't seem to hear. He kept running, stumbling now and then. His clothing steamed steadily in the cold air. One hand slipped on his face, exposing a wide, wild eye staring forward. His cheek looked flatten, as if the skin were pulled tight against the bone. Water dribbled down his face, made it look like his skin was running.

Paul managed to grab Bertie's arm, drag it back, trying to stop him. The hand dropped from his face, exposing the left side. His skin hung off his skull in huge globs. Steam rose from his chin and forehead. The bottom of his eyelid pulled away from his eye, exposing a sliver of white bone.

Paul stumbled in a puddle, his hand slipping off Bertie's arm. Bertie pulled away and fled, ignoring Paul's shouted warning. He raced into the street. A truck's horn blared, screaming with a human voice which sounded strangely like Paul's own as it barreled down on Bertie. Brakes squealed but did little good on the slick pavement. Giant wheels hid Bertie from Paul's sight.

The truck shuddered to a halt thirty feet forward of where Bertie ran into the road. Paul stared at the spot on the road where Bertie had fallen. The rain blurred his gaze and distorted the view of the pile of flesh and bone past any recognizable vision of a man. Around him, the rain continued to fall on the deserted carnival, sounding like hollow applause upon the wooden roofs.

Paul sat at his desk, finishing his notes as he did now every evening, even though he'd only returned to work half days in the last month. His own therapist had advised him to get back into it slowly but he was ready to resume his full schedule. He wouldn't push it though, he knew how easy it would be to overdo it.

Closing the file, Paul collected the few others and took them out to Sharon's desk. She had left for the day but he noticed the archive box under her desk. He opened it, flipped through the names. Stopped at a particular one.

Sadness and frustration flooded him when he saw Bertie's name. They'd come so close to making real progress and then a stupid, unforeseen accident erased it all. Bertie had never had a day free from his fears and obsessions; Paul had never been able to give that to him. He let the box flap drop. A sad smile touched his lips. In a way, Bertie was now free from his obsessions while Paul had to struggle with his own.

You can't save everyone, he thought. Sometimes it's just impossible. He told himself that often, a mantra against the despair. Sometimes it worked.

He gathered his coat from the closet and left the office, turning out the lights. Outside he found the sun blotted out behind a layer of clouds. Funny, he hadn't heard anything about rain today. Turning the collar of his coat up, he headed for the subway.

The wind began to pick up, making his coat flap. Dampness in the air reminded him of Bertie. He tried not to dwell on it but he found himself recalling that night, remembering the rain, the smell of wet earth, the fear in Bertie's eyes.

It knows. Bertie running away in a blind panic, hands covering his face. Paul's stomach churned at the memory. He couldn't change what happened, he wished it wouldn't haunt him so. Bertie's hands red from the cold. The rain streaming off his face, making it look as if it were melting. But it was only water, only the rain, yet in his panicked condition, Bertie fled straight into the road, straight into the path of an eighteen wheel truck.

It's coming. The sky was noticeably darker now, the wind whipping his coat. Paul hunched his shoulders and hurried forward. Only another couple of blocks to the subway and he'd be safe out of the rain. The thought slowed him down. That was an odd thing to think. Why did he think "safe"?

The first few drops caught him by surprise, splashing on his forehead and running into his right eye. He dodged under a restaurant canopy as the rain, sporadically at first, then with increasing force, began to fall.

Paul pressed himself against the wall, watching the sheets of rain fall on the street. Around him, pedestrians rushed to get out of the rain. Others pulled out umbrellas and hurried along. Everyone was afraid of getting wet, like that was anything to be afraid of.

After a moment, he became aware of the pounding of his heart, how his hands clenched at his sides. He forced his fingers to relax, took deep breaths to still his heart. This was ridiculous, it was only rain, only water. Nothing to be afraid of. Bertie had allowed his fear to overwhelm him, to chase him down the street where real danger destroyed him. In a way, the rain had been successful, it had caused Bertie to destroy himself.

It's not going to be successful with me, Paul thought. The subway was a block away.

He buttoned his coat to his chin and pulled leather gloves from his pocket. Rain dripped steadily off the edge of the canopy, spreading a small puddle toward his feet. He wondered something. A silly thought really, but maybe...

His hand reached out. At the edge of the canopy, then beyond. Into the rain.

Water fell on it. Cool. Wet. He smiled, chuckled to himself.

Then laser heat scorched his fingers. He jerked his hand back, cradled it against his chest. The fingers were red, the flesh looked indistinct, edges blurred and running together. Steam rose from the tips. His skin was, oh god, his skin was melting. It knew, *it knew.*

Paul pressed his back against the building, staring out at the waiting rain. The pain in his hand burned white hot as he clutched it. But he didn't move, couldn't take a step. The rain would get him. It had been waiting all this time for him to slip up and now he had.

Fear clenched his spine. How long could he stand here, how long would it last? An hour, a night? Would it ease off to fool him and then come pounding back when he emerged to race for the subway? What could he do?

Paul whimpered in pain and stared out at the rain as it washed the street clean of dirt. One step and it would wash him away. One step. He couldn't move.

In the Walls

Lying in his bed, he could hear them. Soft scratching inside the walls, echoing through the darkness in his bedroom. Tiny nails scraping the drywall, sometimes striking against the metal screws or main wood beams. A scratching that filled the room. But were they actually scraping in the walls? Sometimes he felt it in his head, as if their tiny nails dug into his brain, leaving deep furrows. He could almost see remnants of his gray matter collecting under their nails, drying to a hard, dark crust.

Switching on the light did no good, neither did banging on the walls. They would be silent for a time, then start up again. If not tonight, then tomorrow. He would never be rid of them.

"Stop tossing around, Roger. Go to sleep." Miriam's voice snapped out in the darkness.

"I can't sleep," he said. "The squirrels..."

"Oh for god's sake," she said. "I told you to call the exterminator if they bother you so much. If you aren't going to do it, I'll call them tomorrow. Now go to sleep."

He didn't respond and soon her breathing grew regular and deep. But still over it he could hear them, scratching and scratching, as if something was digging itself out of the grave.

"My husband will be here to meet you," Miriam said into the phone as he entered the kitchen. She nodded sharply and hung up.

"What is that?" he said.

"I called the exterminators," she said. "They'll be here this afternoon. You'll have to stay to meet them. I have an appointment at Raphael's." She slipped on her florescent pink Donna Karan jacket and began buttoning it.

"But I have to go into the office today," he said.

"Call in sick or something," she said. A flip of her hand sent her long brunette hair cascading over her shoulders. "Look, you're the one always complaining about those squirrels. Shall I cancel the exterminators?" She put a hand on the phone. One eyebrow arched in a challenge.

He swallowed. "No, that's fine. I'll wait. I do want to get rid of them."

"Good. That's settled." She slung her purse over her shoulder and scooped up her briefcase. Her lips left a smudge of lipstick on his cheek as she smeared her lips across his skin.

"I'll be home late tonight." Her words trailed back as she walked out the door. "Don't hold dinner."

The car engine starting was a distant rumble that left a vacuum in its wake as she drove away. The house settled into silence around him. He watched the kitchen clock's second hand tick away but couldn't hear it. He strained to hear the scraping but there was nothing. It was too early for that.

Calling the office, he faked illness, coughing elaborately into the phone. Hanging up, he knew they wouldn't be convinced. Yet another mark against him at the office. Naturally Miriam couldn't wait for the exterminators. Somehow her part time job had turned out to have more hours than his full time one and was deemed to be worth a whole new wardrobe while he had to make do with five-year-old suits.

Well, maybe he could catch up on some paperwork. He'd left his briefcase in the family room and when he fetched it he realized by the lightness that he'd left his laptop at the office. Typical. Of course he'd packed all his disks but managed to leave the computer behind.

Miriam had set up an office in the attic, complete with a desktop machine and a DSL line. She'd forbidden him from using it but she was going to be late, and if he couldn't get into the office because of the exterminator, she certainly couldn't begrudge him a few hours on the computer.

The office was pure Miriam, colored in cream, beige and pink. Only the best in office furniture because ergonomics was so important, but she barely spent any time here. How had he been relegated to the basement?

Sunlight from the attic window warmed the room. When he sat down, he found the sun reflected squarely onto the screen. Several minutes flew by as he adjusted the angle. Now finally.

He turned on the machine, reaching for his disks as the computer booted itself up. He definitely had to get some work done on the Carmichael file.

He sat up straight in the chair and his head brushed the wall. Of course, in the attic, the walls sloped sharply toward the ceiling. Miriam was shorter than him and would be fine where he bumped his head.

More minutes passed as he shuffled the desk

forward until he could sit without brushing his head. He stared at the beige wall. Just behind there the squirrels were lurking, just waiting to start their scratching and scratching. How long would they have to work until they broke through? Maybe they would break through to Miriam's precious attic office. He could picture their tiny nails tearing through the paint, paws reaching in to pull them through the widening hole, invading this dust free space with their muddy prints, trailing fur and dirt in their tracks. He imagined them running up the walls, even along the ceiling as if defying gravity, defying Miriam.

Suddenly he didn't want the exterminators to come.

He found the number where Miriam had marked it in the phone book and for the first time he was glad she always made little pen stars beside the places she called. His fingers trembled as he punched in the number. A metallic ringing began in his ear.

"Hendersons' Exterminators."

"Ah, yes, I have an appointment this afternoon that I need to cancel."

"Certainly. Do you wish to reschedule?"

"Um no, not at this time. That's fine."

"There is a fifty dollar cancellation fee for canceling within twenty-four hours."

His heart beat a little faster. "That's fine."

"Your name and address, sir?"

He gave her all the pertinent information and hung up. He'd done it. Cancelled the exterminators. A perverse thrill quivered through his body. He would tell Miriam the exterminators came. She would never imagine that he'd cancelled them.

If he wanted, he could go to the office and for a moment he thought he would do that, then he remembered. He was supposed to be sick. Sure, they probably realized he'd lied but he couldn't very well show up looking completely healthy. He would go back tomorrow.

He returned to Miriam's office in the attic. The beige walls and cream furniture seemed warmer to him. With the desk farther from the wall, he could slide in behind it in comfort. He inserted the Carmichael disk into the laptop. Sunlight streamed through the windows, improving his mood even more. He whistled as he worked.

He didn't realize the time until his stomach started rumbling. God, it was almost seven! He hadn't eaten anything since breakfast. Heading for the kitchen, he remembered Miriam telling him not to hold dinner. Well, he certainly wasn't waiting for her now.

Freed from her picky appetite, he grilled himself a steak with a potato wrapped in tin foil. Mushrooms fried in butter and some garlic bread with melted cheese completed the meal. He opened a beer and drank it straight from the bottle. Why bother dirtying up a glass?

Leaving the used dishes in the sink, he settled in to watch the game on television, remote in one hand, another beer in the other. Around him he felt the emptiness of the house, comforting. But it wasn't completely empty. Somewhere the squirrels were waiting to start their scratching, waiting to break through. He smiled.

He fell asleep in front of the TV, waking to the gray swirl of a dead channel. Had Miriam come home? He turned the TV off, staring blurrily at the time. Two thirty. His body felt old and creaky as he climbed out of the easy chair and made his way to the bedroom. As his eyes adjusted to the gloom, he saw her shape under the bed covers. She had come home, she just hadn't bothered to wake him. And why would she? It wasn't like she'd wanted him in bed. This way she got all the covers.

Then he heard it, the scratching. Rhythmic. Even. He stood in the doorway, transfixed. How far in were they now? Would they break through the wall in the attic any moment? His heartbeat quickened at the thought. Maybe he should wake Miriam, flaunt his disobedience in her face. The scratching stopped. His breath caught in his throat. What happened? Where were the squirrels? Come back, he thought, come back. He wanted them scratching, he needed them to scratch, to tear through the drywall, tiny nails digging at the glue of the wallpaper, ripping the cream paint in the attic, tearing through her flesh.

The scratching started again and he could breathe. They didn't want him to wake Miriam, he realized. Not yet. They weren't ready for her, they weren't close enough to the attic. In a few days, yes, they would be closer in a few days. He could hear it in the scratching, in the rhythm. They were telling him all he needed to know.

<hr>

"So the exterminators came yesterday?" she asked him at breakfast.

He took a sip of his coffee, making her wait for his answer. Her pink polished nails drummed on the table in front of him. She sighed heavily.

"Well, Roger, did they come?"

"Yes, Miriam. The exterminators came."

"So? Are you satisfied?"

"Yes, Miriam. I'm very happy."

"Good, now we won't have any more nonsense about the damned squirrels." She stood up from the table, brushing nonexistent crumbs from her skirt. "I have to work late again tonight. Try not to fall asleep in front of the TV this time."

"Yes dear," he said. Her heels clicked on the tile as she walked down the hall to the door. It reminded him of the squirrels scratching.

In the office, everyone said they were glad to see him feeling better. He knew from their overly cheerful smiles that they didn't mean it but he didn't care. He plunged into work and by noon had filled his out tray. His secretary had to empty it twice.

"You should get sick more often," she said. "It really gets you going."

He gave her a huge smile and told her to take lunch, hell, take an extra half hour. Clutching the files, she gaped at him then smiled back. "Thanks, Roger."

He ate lunch at his desk and was halfway through his sandwich when he heard the scratching, soft, distant. Had they followed him? He paused mid-chew, listening. Yes, there it was, letting him know he was doing well, letting him know they were happy with him. While he was being industrious at work, they were doing their part at home, getting closer and closer to the attic. He wondered if he'd be able to see their progress in the walls. Closing his eyes, he could imagine them behind the drywall. Tiny nails poked out from beneath the fur of their paws. Black eyes stared at the wall, the obstacle, concentrating. Muscles in their arms flexed as they dug. Back legs worked at pushing the loosened debris back out of the way. He could see the layer of fine white dust covering their black fur. Maybe one of them was a grey squirrel. Another a brown one. He liked that idea, that there were several of them, each a different color, working together, moving ever closer to the attic.

Then he imagined Miriam in the attic, just at the moment they broke through. First her look of astonishment, then the perpetual look of annoyance that was her everyday face, finally dissolving to horror as they leapt at her with their digging claws.

He opened his eyes. He felt flushed and excited. His clenching hands had creased several reports. He released them, smoothing their surface. Remain calm, he had to remain calm. No sense getting all riled when they weren't close to the attic just yet. Several deep breaths slowed his racing heart.

After work when he arrived home, he went straight upstairs to see if he could spot any progress. In the silence, he studied the walls carefully, noting the slight color variation in the paint, a brief ripple in the wallpaper. Nothing to indicate squirrel activity. Disappointment made his shoulders sag. He knew he shouldn't get his hopes up. He knew he had to be more patient. They would come in their own time.

He ate dinner and watched a couple of TV shows before heading to bed. Of course, Miriam wasn't home yet. He lay awake, listening for scratching. Silence.

She came home around eleven thirty. He pretended to be asleep as she crept into the room and slid under the covers beside him. He lay very still, listening to her breathe, waiting for it to deepen into sleep. Finally when it did, he slipped out of the bed and out of the room.

Gloom filled the attic. The window faced

the street and a lone streetlight but even that light seemed dull and dark. He could see in the darkness. He hadn't bothered to turn on the lights to come up. He felt like he could move anywhere in the dark.

Odd how the room looked at night. He hadn't thought it would appear so different. When he thought of the attic he always thought of it as Miriam's domain, drenched in her colors, her fussiness. But at night it was quite different.

At night, the room seemed its own. No longer hidden by the false gaiety of Miriam's decoration, it revealed its true nature of shadow and darkness. He could imagine boxes of memories stored here, hiding from the light. Secrets and dreams forgotten. But the room never forgot. It would not tell its secrets, neither would it forget them. It had held wisdom behind the perversion of its decor.

Then he heard it. Faint, distant. Scratching in the walls. He moved to the center of the room, tried to guess which wall they were coming from. He couldn't. He scrambled to press his ear to each wall. A chair leapt in his way, making him stumble. As he righted himself, the scratching stopped.

He froze, held his breath. They wouldn't have left, they couldn't have left. Damn chair getting in his way. He'd startled them, was all. Any moment they would start again.

His lungs ached, reminding him to breathe. He did so as quietly as possible, still waiting. Hours dragged back or was it only seconds? Would they have left? Would they have taken his being in the room as a lack of faith and decided he was unworthy? Despair weighed on his shoulders, pressing them downward. He wanted to sink into the floor.

Scratching. He caught his breath. Yes, there it was! Tears came to his eyes. They had not abandoned him. He had only startled them and now weren't they actually scratching harder? Knowing he was waiting for them, were they not working faster?

He pressed his ear to the wall beside the computer desk. Yes, this was where they would come in. Another few days. He could hear it in the rhythm of their digging. He would be ready.

Silently he crept from the attic and back to bed.

"What's the matter with you?" Miriam asked.

He stopped whistling as he poured his morning coffee. "Nothing. Why?"

Her eyebrows arched at him. "You are acting very strange. Whistling and cheerful. What's going on?"

His hand trembled at the suspicion in her voice. Don't spill the coffee. He set the carafe down.

"I'm just glad to be having a good night's sleep is all," he said.

"Oh really?" Her eyes narrowed as she studied him. "You don't look like you're sleeping well. You've got bags under your eyes."

He fought the urge to touch his face. "Bags? Really?" He forced a laugh, then stopped as her frown deepened. "I feel quite well rested."

"Are you sure? I don't want to hear complaints about squirrels keeping you up again. Are you sure the exterminators got every one of them?"

He took a deep breath. Did she suspect he'd lied about the exterminators? He couldn't let her call them, couldn't let her know he'd been up in the night, listening to the scratching, waiting.

"There's some tight deadlines at work, but we're on top of them. Now that I'm sleeping better I know it'll work out."

At the mention of his job, her gaze glazed over. He knew she hated to hear about his work although she felt compelled to tell him every detail of her part time job. Funny, she hadn't mentioned much about it lately.

She turned her attention back to her magazine. He drank his coffee, careful not to whistle. He would have to make sure he didn't act too happy. He couldn't let her know they were coming. She would call the exterminators on them.

That thought almost set his hands trembling again but he controlled them. He remembered them scratching in the walls, working harder when they realized he was there, waiting faithfully. They knew he had cancelled the exterminators that Miriam had called. They trusted him. He believed in them and it steadied him.

When he finished his coffee, he rinsed the cup and left it in the sink. As he bent to kiss Miriam on the cheek, she pulled away.

"Can't you put the cup in the dishwasher just once?"

"Sorry, dear." He had thought of putting it directly in the dishwasher, but that would have been unusual. From now on, everything he did had to be the same old thing.

He put the cup in the dishwasher and this time, she allowed him to kiss her cheek.

"Are you working late tonight, dear?" he asked.

"Of course not, Roger. You know it's Wednesday and I have group on Wednesday."

"Of course. See you later."

He escaped into the sunshine and the safety of his car where he could whistle all he wanted.

For the next three nights, he waited for Miriam to fall asleep before creeping up to the attic. He sat on the floor, listening to the scratching, hearing how they had progressed from one night to the next. He didn't speak to them. They were animals, they didn't know human English, but they did understand thoughts, feelings. He could feel how they understood him, understood all he'd been through and how he needed them. He could hear how they worked faster while he sat there, as if they were performing especially for him. When he wasn't there, he knew they worked half-heartedly, as if it wasn't worth it. He understood that. They needed him as much as he needed them. So he stayed up longer each night, listening to them, drawing them closer with his thoughts.

In the mornings he struggled to maintain the usual routine. Miriam seemed to no longer notice the bags under his eyes, not surprising as she barely looked at him at the best of times. He found he wanted a second cup after his coffee at home but he couldn't risk changing the routine. She might question him farther and figure out about the exterminators. He began stopping for a second coffee on the way to work, then grabbing another when he got there. The caffeine made him jittery but allowed him to function throughout the day. He ignored the questioning glances of his secretary and coworkers.

His work suffered. But it was only temporary, everything would be all right once they broke through the wall. Of course, he couldn't tell anyone about that, they wouldn't understand. So he stayed silent and did the best he could, always wishing he could stay home and sit in the attic instead of sitting in this damned stupid office chair.

Saturday was more of a challenge. It was their "together" day but when he got up, he found a note from Miriam saying she'd gone to a special antiques show with Gail and would be home for dinner. Perfect. He could spend most of the day in the attic.

After a quick shower, he toasted a bagel and made a carafe of coffee, carrying it all upstairs with him. Sunlight poured through the window, chasing away the comforting shadows of the night. Strange to be in the attic in the daylight. He had gotten so used to it at night.

He sat on the floor with his coffee and bagel. He ate and drank quietly but there was no scratching. Did they not realize he was here? He frowned. Had they lost faith in him? Had he done something to upset them? He reviewed his actions of the last week. He had done everything possible to make it easier for them. Hadn't he shown his devotion?

Perhaps they needed to see that he was willing to meet them halfway. Of course! He raced out of the room, down the stairs. In the garage he kept their gardening tools. For a time Miriam had tended the backyard garden but now her part-time job took up too much of her time. The tools had been left to rust in the garage.

He found the one he'd been looking for. A large multi-pronged tiller, the blades curved to make it easier to dig in the ground. He could already hear it scratching on the wall.

Back in the attic, he tested it on the wall behind the desk, timid at first, then with increasing confidence. The paint flaked under the claw of the tiller, then peeled away. Sweat beaded on his forehead, dripped into his eyes. He swiped it away, kept working. The sunlight beat onto his back, its movement throwing his shadow into a dance around his work. The hole widened. Dust made him sneeze, teared his eyes. He kept working. He didn't realize the sun had gone down until it was dark.

He stopped. The tiller dropped from his numb fingers. Without looking at the wall, he stumbled out of the room to the bathroom. Under the spray of the shower, he felt the dust from the wall drain away, leaving his muscles tingling. It almost felt like his skin was draining away with the dust as if the act of scratching through the walls was a way of being reborn. He laughed aloud.

In the kitchen, he rummaged in the fridge for food. The answering machine winked at him. He hit the play button. A message from Miriam; she was staying for dinner with Gail. Had the phone rung? He couldn't remember hearing it.

The food was tasteless but nourishing. He slipped the dish into the dishwasher. His back ached as he stood and he was suddenly aware of the fatigue in his arms and shoulders. He had to nap, surely they would understand if he slept for a few hours. He stumbled up to the bedroom and fell into bed.

He awoke at three in the morning. Miriam lay beside him, turned away on her side. Lying in the bed, he could hear them. Soft scratching inside the walls, echoing through the darkness in his bedroom. His heart sped up in his chest. Soon! He slid out of bed, careful not to wake Miriam, and crept up to the attic.

Now the gloom was comforting and familiar. He stared at the wall behind the computer desk, amazed at the work he had done. The hole was huge, as tall as he was and almost half as wide. The sound of their scratching was loud now. Each hammer of their nails filled the room. He picked up the tiller and clutched it to his chest. Tonight. He knew they would come tonight.

The light flared on, blinding him.

"What the hell?" Miriam's voice shrieked, drowning out the scratching.

He turned, blinking madly to clear the tears from his eyes.

"Roger, what in god's name is going on here?

What happened to my wall?" Her voice rose even louder.

He trembled. The scratching had stopped. They knew she was here, knew he had failed them. Now they would never come and he would never be free.

"I cancelled the exterminators," he whispered.

"What?" she shouted. "What about the wall? There's dust all over my computer!"

"The squirrels," he said. Saying it aloud gave him strength. He raised his voice. "They're coming. The squirrels."

"Roger, you are crazy. I'm calling the exterminators in the morning, then someone to fix my wall and then a doctor to get you committed."

She turned away and the scratching began. Louder than anything. Their nails sharp as steel, curved and multi-pronged. She tried to scream but the scratching was louder and stronger. She was easier to dig through than the wall, no paint flaking or dust getting in his eyes. Sometimes the tiller caught on bone or got bogged down in flesh. All he had to do was give a mighty wrench and it came free. Hands groped at him but fell away soon enough. Then her screaming faded and all that was left was the scratching, tiny nails scraping, filling the room and he found, with effort, he could dig his way out.

These Premises Protected By...

"I told you the back door was the easiest," Denny Wilson said, drawing the kitchen shades. "I've been walking this neighborhood for months."

His partner, Billy Wayne Benton, stood inside the door, his hefty six foot four inch frame hiding the ruined door jam. He hated when Denny bragged about his methods, especially during a job. Excess talking was sloppy, a sign of inferior thinking. Billy didn't talk unless absolutely necessary.

This habit suited Denny perfectly. His short, lithe body skimmed across the tile floor and he peeked into the dining room. More windows, these blinds drawn but not totally closed.

"Wait here," he told Billy. He could see the man nod impatiently, a flicker of distaste crossing his face. Denny grinned. He loved to needle the big, silent man.

He toured the bottom floor of the house, posh living room, exquisite dining room, crisp office/den. Taping the edges of the shades with masking tape, he mumbled as the double thick gloves stuck on the tape. He'd read once that cops could get prints through thin gloves and he'd doubled up ever since.

Finishing, he returned to the stark, white kitchen where Billy waited.

"All ready, your highness."

Billy snorted and pushed past him, one hand brushing Denny's sleeve. Denny noticed that his glove was thin. Obviously Billy hadn't read the same article.

They worked methodically, room by room.

Denny stacked stereo equipment by the back door. He preferred taking everything out to the van at once, instead of piecemeal as they went along. It was cleaner, neater. Looked more like a move than a robbery.

The sound of drawers opening told Denny that Billy was in the dining room. The big man definitely had a flare for silver, being able to distinguish the real thing from cheap stainless steel with barely a glance. It almost made up for his personality, his brooding silences and nasty glares. They'd never be friends but Denny knew the value of a working relationship.

The 42 inch LCD panel television proved too heavy for him to lift. He retreated to the office/ den where Billy was rifling a rollup desk.

"Can you get the TV?" Denny said. "Too heavy for me."

Billy nodded, a sharp movement of his large head. His hair, cut to an inch, barely shifted. He eased the cover down and slipped out from behind the desk. He had remarkably grace for all his bulk. Denny remembered how he had elegantly pulverized the biker at the bar last Wednesday who kept interrupting their final plans for this job.

Of course, such bulk made Billy stand out, made him noticeable in a crowd, around a neighborhood. He couldn't pick houses for himself. That was Denny's job. Nondescript, inconspicuous Denny, who could fit in with mechanics or bankers, depending on his clothes and attitude. His mother's always said he could've been a great actor, just like Sir Larry, but Denny knew just how much most actors ever made.

Forget that.

With a grunt, Billy hefted the LCD panel television. He inched toward the doorway. Denny stepped out into the hallway watching. Billy's feet sank into the plush white carpet as he moved forward, his thick treads leaving deep marks like a golfer's treads in virgin green.

"Easy now," Denny murmured.

Billy stepped into the hallway, heading for the kitchen two dozen or so paces away. Denny tiptoed behind.

Almost to the kitchen, he was breathing a

sigh of relief. Billy moved confidently, now used to the television's weight. He strode down the hallway and as one foot stepped onto the kitchen tile, the other, resting on the carpet, began to rise. Suddenly his foot pulled back, slipping on the rug. With a yell, the big man began to fall. He twisted, arms pushing the television away. The unit hit the wall with a crash as the screen exploded. Billy landed on his side, his face a few inches from the ruined set.

"Shit, Billy." Denny rushed forward, reaching down to help the big man stand but Billy slapped his hands away. Billy's face was blotchy and red.

"Why'd you pull at the carpet?" he growled.

"What? What the hell are you talking about? I didn't pull at the carpet. You slipped."

"The carpet was pulled out from under my foot," Billy roared.

"Shut up, you want the neighbors to hear you?" Denny shook his head. "Why the hell would I pull the carpet? You think I wanted to destroy the television? That's three maybe four hundred dollars gone. Do I look stupid?"

Slowly the color settled in Billy's face. He

glared at the offending carpeting. One foot poked at it cautiously.

"Look it's just carpet. We're lucky the screen didn't land on you."

Billy grunted.

"Come on," Denny urged. "Let's finish up this floor. Forget that." He gestured vaguely to the ruined tv.

They abandoned the television in the hallway, retreating to the office. Billy returned to the rollup desk, absently rubbing his hip. Denny scanned the bookshelves that flanked the heavily curtained window. After a moment, he noticed how many of the books dealt with parapsychology. Jez, these people actually had the whole Time/Life set. He remembered watching those stupid commercials at four in the morning, nursing the beginnings of a hangover.

He tapped one of the bindings. "Hey, Billy, what's lycanthropy?"

"Werewolves," Billy murmured.

Denny snorted. "Like 'American Werewolf in London'". He'd liked that movie, funny. These people seemed to actually believe it. Some people believed anything these days.

His fingers explored the bindings of the books and sure enough, a different kind of pressure on the shelf just above his head. He grabbed a handful of books and tossed then to the floor. Groping around on the shelves, his fingertips brushed the sharp edges of paper. He grabbed and pulled out a large brown envelope. Bingo, the family cookie jar. He ripped open the envelope and rifled through the bills, mostly twenties. Just over five hundred, he figured. Rainy day money. Sorry, folks, it just started pouring.

He turned to wave the money at Billy. A scrapping sound made him hesitate. He started to turn back.

A book smacked him hard on his head.

Yelping, Denny jumped back. The book landed on the grey carpeting, pages splaying open. His head was sore where the book hit him, already he could feel a bruise starting.

"Son of a bitch," he said, rubbing the spot.

"You should be more careful how you treat

books," Billy said wryly as he stooped to pick up the money Denny had dropped.

"How could that hit me?" the little man said. He glanced back at the bookcase.

"You must have moved it too close to the edge." Billy stuffed the bills back into the envelope and folded it. As Denny watched, the envelope disappeared inside Billy's jacket. Denny started to protest but then thought better of it. Billy was almost a foot taller and at least forty pounds heavier than he was. Besides, cheating your partner was not good business, it got you a reputation and soon no one would work with you. Billy was too smart to make that mistake.

"Anything in the desk?" he asked.

Billy shook his head. "Just papers, family records. Nothing for us."

"Let's check the upstairs."

They moved up the stairs, Denny trailing one hand along the polished wooden banister. Very elegant looking, he thought. But he couldn't really appreciate it. His head was starting to throb from where the book hit him. Maybe he'd find some aspirin in the bathroom medicine cabinet.

"Let's get the jewelry first," he said to Billy. "We can get the portable stereos and shit later."

Billy's curt nod was his only answer as they moved to the master bedroom. After Denny taped the curtains shut, Billy slipped over to the dresser, his big hands plunging into the jewelry box.

Denny started over to help but got distracted by a large full year calendar tacked up to the closet door. That looked odd. Most people kept this sort of thing in a den or something. He traced the dates with one gloved hand. Three or four days were circled in red every month, notations made for each one: "Grandma's," "Holiday Inn," "McGregor's," "Bed and breakfast." Looks like they go away every month, he thought. He should copy down the dates. In six months or so, after the insurance claims were settled, they could return. The cops would tell the residents that robbers won't return and then he and Billy could strike again.

He pulled out an old bus schedule and started scribbling down dates. After a few, he noticed a pattern.

"Hey Billy," he called. "Look at this. These people go away every month on the full moon. Maybe one of them is a werewolf."

A rare grin broke through the usual bland expression on Billy's face. He lifted a gold chain and wagged it at Denny. "I might've known, none of this stuff is silver."

Denny chuckled. He liked that. After copying a few more dates, he stuffed the schedule back into his pocket. While Billy finished with the jewelry box, dumping selected items into a canvas bag, Denny commenced to scour the drawers. Systematically, he pulled out every drawer and dumped the contents on the bed. Clothes mostly, with little bags of pot pourri to smell it up nicely. He turned over the drawers, looking for anything taped to the bottom. He'd broken into one place and found money taped to the bottom of every drawer in the bureau and ever since then he checked methodically.

Nothing. Should've known. He left the drawers and the mound of clothes on the bed. He opened the closet, door, barely glancing at the yearly calendar. He was stretching his thin frame to its full height when the lights went out.

"What the hell?" Billy's voice snarled in the sudden darkness. Denny couldn't see anything. He couldn't have done that good a job taping the curtains to the wall. Surely a sliver of light would get in from the streetlights outside. But the darkness was heavy and oppressive, pressing against him even though he knew the bedroom was large, the furniture widely spaced.

"Probably some kinda timer," he said, louder than necessary just to hear his own voice. Billy, he knew, was across the room, but other than the first exclamation he couldn't detect the big man's presence.

Carefully Denny stretched out his hand, feeling the closet door under his fingertips. He followed it along to the wall and used the wall to lead him to where he thought the door should be. Naturally he'd left his flashlight downstairs.

He could picture it sitting on the kitchen counter beside the backdoor. Shouldn't be too hard to get but he cursed the amount of time this would take up. He wanted to be out of here before sunrise.

The wall felt like some kind of stucco, scrapping against his fingertips. Jesus, it was taking a long time to get to the door. Had he turned the wrong way and was heading toward the bed? Just his luck, he'd end up banging his shins and have to turn around to start again.

"Hey Billy, I'm going for the flashlight," he said. Nothing came back out of the darkness. No noise, no feeling of movement. Had Billy gone ahead and left the room already? No, impossible, he would hear the big man's plodding footsteps down the stairs. But the darkness was perfectly silent, absorbing the sound of his movements like a drop of water into a well. It pressed against him, making it hard to breathe except in shallow, short gasps. Where the hell was Billy, he wondered. When would he reach the door?

He wasn't going to panic, he told himself. He was a professional, he'd picked locks in darkness like this, worked jobs in minimal light. He'd never had a problem with darkness, not even as a kid, and he wasn't about to have one now.

Purposely, he took a step and then another. He was probably right by the door now, any minute he'd feel the frame beneath his questing fingers. Any second.

His trailing fingers suddenly sank into something wet and lumpy. What? Oatmeal, was the first thought in his mind, dredged up from some long forgotten motherly attempt by his aunt to feed him. But that was impossible, he was touching the wall.

Maybe some weird renovation, he thought. Never mind that there hadn't been anything wrong with the wall when he'd walked in with Billy, never mind that it didn't make sense for a wall to suddenly turn fluid. He wouldn't allow for any other thought.

Keep going, there'll be drywall. He pulled his hand out of the muck, letting his fingertips brush lightly along. The door, he was heading for the door.

Then the carpeting beneath his feet felt strange. It had been a grey, tight weave with an abstract etched design working through it. Ordinary, barely noticeable. Firm beneath his shoes. Except now it felt squishy, like he was walking across the surface of a waterbed filled with gelatin. He could feel it move beneath his feet, rolling first to the right and then the left. Balancing became a new trick but still he kept trying to walk forward. It was just the darkness making him edgy, that was all.

But no matter what happened, he did not want to fall over.

Slowly he became aware that the darkness was no longer completely silent. A low creaking, just on the edge of hearing, had started. He couldn't tell where it was coming from, it seemed to hang in the air around him.

"Billy," he called. The word was swallowed by the darkness, by the rising sound that now sounded like the wind or a moan. Yes, that was it. A low moan. Could it be Billy? He strained to listen to it, to distinguish anything meaningful from it. But nothing occurred to him, except the hollow sinking feeling of decay.

Stop it, he told himself. It's just the wind slipping in through a loose window or something. The floor was solid and so was the wall. He'd reached the door any second now.

The moan rose, changing pitch, becoming sharp and harsh, gaining volume, sounding like... like...

A howl.

A high pitched shriek cut across the howl and loud thumps sounded off to his left. Suddenly the wall was gone, not even the mushy oatmeal-like texture anymore. Denny felt the door frame at his fingertips and he clung to it.

"Billy," he cried. The howl swallowed his words, the sound shaping around it to mock him. Then the lights sprang on, full brightness, blinding him. He rubbed at his eyes, tears leaking from the corners. The howl screeched in his ears, rising to a wail.

Billy!

Still blinking, Denny opened his eyes. The

stairs on the right curved downward, their edges sharp and foreboding. Gingerly, he crossed to stand at the top and stare at the heap at the bottom.

For a moment, he thought of laundry because of the way the clothes were twisted, but he spotted an arm poking this way, a leg that way. Billy wailed again.

Denny grabbed the rail and began to descend. Every step brought him closer, every step made him wonder how could a body be twisted like that? Falling down the stairs in the dark wouldn't do it, but that's what had to have happened. Billy must've fallen.

His hand grasped the big man's shoulder, as if Denny needed to assure himself of Billy's physical reality. The muscle quivered beneath his fingertips. Billy moaned again.

"It's okay, Billy." Denny's voice sounded weak and uncertain, even to his own ears. He cleared his throat. "You must've just slipped in the dark."

Carefully, he worked at straightening his partner's body, no longer caring if his wails brought the police running. Billy's limbs splayed at unnatural angles. His face was twisted and red with pain. Tears coursed down his cheeks. His lips trembled, words coming too softly for Denny to hear. Stooping, he pressed his ear close to Billy's lips.

"Didn't fall, something grabbed," the big man gasped. His voice faded and he breathed heavily through his mouth as though the four words had drained all his strength.

Denny remembered the howl, thought about the oatmeal wall, but that was just craziness, just fantasy, just the dark getting on his nerves. To admit anything else was too big a step for someone as pragmatic as Denny to take. He didn't believe in the bogeyman, didn't believe in haunted houses or vampires or anything like Freddie Kruger. That was movies, make believe.

"There's nobody else here," he said. He forced a confidence he didn't feel into his voice. "You just fell, but don't worry. I'll get you outta here. It'll be all right."

Billy tried to whisper something else but

Denny didn't bend down to hear it. He walked toward the kitchen, keeping his pace sure and even. It was an effort not to run.

With Billy as badly wounded as Denny suspected, the job was finished. They'd barely got started, he thought bitterly, but there was no use whining about it. Right now they had to get out and count their blessings.

The back door was properly shut, the ruined lock gapping like a wound. On the waist-high counter along the wall lay the flashlight, just where he'd thought it would be. For reassurance, Denny hefted it in his hand. The best thing to do now would be to get out, take Billy somewhere. He knew people who could help and they didn't ask questions like a hospital would.

He grabbed the door knob and twisted. The knob slid though his fingers, feeling as substantial as gelatin. He tried again. Still he couldn't get a grip, but that didn't matter, the lock was ruined so the door should swing open. He kicked it, expecting it to rebound back. Instead the wood indented, as if made of rubber, then slowly resumed its shape.

Denny's heart pounded inside his thin chest. The door was stuck, something in the lock jammed; that was it. His fingers searched the edges, prying between the door and the door frame. But he couldn't get a grip, couldn't even slip his fingers between the seams. And there had to be seams, it was a door, for god's sake. But his fingers found only a solid seal as if the door had melded to the wall.

"Godammit!" Denny yelled. He pulled out the flashlight and began pounding on the door. Billy's scream stopped him.

Denny froze, the flashlight drooping in his fingers. Billy cried out again, calling to him.

"Denny, help!"

He didn't want to, didn't care anymore about the job or his reputation or his working relationship with Billy. He just wanted out. Billy's scream came again, tightening the skin across Denny's scalp. He clenched the flashlight and crossed to the kitchen door.

The hallway was brightly lit, showing how far Billy had managed to drag his ruined body before he'd stopped, or was stopped. He'd raised himself up on one hand, the other reaching for the wall for support. But Denny could see that Billy was trying to pull away from the wall, could see where his hand disappeared into the flowered wallpaper. A red stain spread over the patterned flowers, and Denny caught a glimpse of bone as Billy jerked away from the wall. His arm suddenly came free, a stump spraying blood where his hand had been. Denny noticed hunks of flesh hanging on the wall. Slowly, they disappeared, as if the wall was absorbing them. Then the stain faded, leaving the flowered wallpaper intact and clean.

Billy fell forward on the hallway throw-rugs, the stump extending toward Denny. Blood pulsed out, soaking into the plush fabric. Billy's eyes rolled up, exposing the whites. He sagged, unconscious. Then his body began rocking and Denny thought he'd been wrong and Billy wasn't unconscious. But as he watched, the pile began shifting, as though blown by an unfelt wind. The pattern of the movement became more like mulching, the edges of the carpet spiking up like teeth. Denny shook his head as the sound of crunching and squishing filled the hallway. Billy's body quivered as the edges of the carpet pierced his skin. As Denny watched, the carpet teeth ground in and Billy began to relax, his body slumping heavier on the carpet. A stain of pinky red and frothy white spread over the fabric, dotted with pieces of Billy's clothes. Dissolving, Denny realized in horror. Billy never regained consciousness as the carpet slowly ate him. The last thing Denny saw was Billy's hand, fingers extended as though reaching for him, before the rug ground it up with the rest. As with the wall, the stain was slowly absorbed.

I'm next, thought Denny wildly. Shit, I'm next!

He ran back to the kitchen but the door was still sealed. Frantically, he pounded on the windows but even the sounds of his pounding were absorbed, muffled. No one outside would be able to hear him.

Keep moving, he thought. He ran through to the dining room and tried to pry the masking tape from the shades, but they too were sealed like the kitchen door. He didn't waste any more time with them and ran into the living room. The windows were the same. He wandered back through the office and remembered the calendar, the circled dates. Today was one of those dates. Had he foolishly thought of coming back here to rob the place again? He'd give anything just to get out now. Then he remembered the pattern of the dates. All the circles were around the time of the full moon. He remembered questioning Billy about lycanthropy. But it wasn't the occupants who were werewolves, it was the house. It was a were-house.

No, that was just crazy.

So was watching your partner being eaten by carpeting.

A prickling sensation on his ankles made him look down. An electric cord wrapped around his pants' leg; was that thorns he saw sticking into the fabric? He tried to pull away. The cord grew taunt and he fell, knocking over a small end table. A potted fern crashed to the carpet beside him. The water made a damp stain by his head.

Fear coursed through Denny. He rolled onto

his back and clawed at the cord. It wrapped tighter and he felt his foot fall asleep. Pins and needles started up his calf and thigh. The cord was digging deeper into his pants, into his leg. He felt his skin fray and break, blood oozed over the fabric and dripped on the carpet. It disappeared almost as it hit the pile, as though the carpet was licking it up.

"Let me go!" Denny shouted. "I won't come back, I promise. Just let me go!"

He clawed for the door frame and as his fingers reached the edges of it, the lights went out for good. The creaking started again, building up to another howl. The house wasn't listening anymore.

"Look honey, there's another van in the driveway." The wife pointed as they pulled up in front of the house.

"I guess you were right about that guy who was looking at the house the last couple of months." The husband turned off the ignition.

"Will the bad men be inside the house, mom?" A blonde haired, six year old girl peered over the back seat.

"No dear, they'll be gone." She exchanged a look with her husband. "The house will have taken care of them. Why don't we take our bags back into the house while Daddy gets rid of the van?"

She opened the passenger door. "Looks like a nice van," her husband said. "I bet I'll get more for it than the last one."

The wife smiled as she started to hustle the children toward the front door. "Just don't forget carpet cleaner this time. It always smells so damp when we've been gone."

The husband nodded as he walked up the driveway toward the van. "I'll get pine scented. The house seems to like that."

Returning Home

The naked bulb of the basement light stung her eyes as Katherine Snelman clutched the slim piece of paper in her hands. The postmark on the envelope read September of the year before, seven months before her mother's death. It seemed impossible, her mother had never told her about this letter, had never hardly mentioned her father, yet the proof was in her trembling hands.

"My dearest Angela,
Although it has been over thirty years since I last saw you, I think of you often. For so long

I have respected your wishes, allowed you to live the life you wanted, now I ask that I be allowed to become a part of it again.

Remember how we danced at the Wonderland Gardens? The sweet smell of roses still brings your face to my mind. I know you must think of me and wonder. Wonder no more!

I will be on the footbridge to the park at midnight on the seventh. I would like to see you, even if only to see you. Please come.
Daniel"

Her hand shook as she brushed the mousy brown bangs out of her eyes. She'd been slowly sorting through her mother's correspondence the past three months, living and reliving the last painful months, the many weekends she'd spent on the road from Toronto to London, visiting her mother, watching as she slipped ever farther away. Her mother had always been proud, even toward the end, refusing hospitalization and arguing with the doctors. Tears stung Katherine's eyes; so typical of her.

Had she gone to meet him, she wondered. At midnight, for god's sake! The footbridge was at least a mile away on the far end of the golf course. On this side of the river it sat at the end of a steep, tree lined road that branched to the footbridge one way and the golf course another. On the other side of the river was Springbank Park, a beautiful rolling park of trees and grass and flowers. But closer to the footbridge, the park gave way to more wild growth of dense underbrush and gnarly trees.

Oh, this was ridiculous, she was getting all worried and upset as if her mother could get hurt now. This was a letter from the past, albeit a strange one. Her mother had probably kept it out of sentiment, not telling her because she knew it would only hurt Katherine; being reminded of a father who had abandoned them. God knows at her age her mother wouldn't have gone down there.

She wanted to throw out the letter, but her hand, having a mind of its own, placed it on a stack of boxes beside the garbage bag. She picked up the shoe box, determined to forget about the letter, and continued to sort through the papers. Bills and more bills. Invitations to join the Book-of-the-Month club. Requests from Save the Children. She tossed it all.

Occasionally her hand brushed the letter. By accident. Her eyes flicked over to see it, to ensure its reality. The paper lay on the boxes, slightly wrinkled. An innocent timebomb.

Suddenly she had to go there, to stand where her father had stood, waiting for her mother. Had he leaned against the rusting rail, green paint dulled by the sun, flaking beneath his elbow? What had he looked like? His features probably would have been as hard to discern in the moonlight as in the old faded picture her mother had kept.

Katherine set the shoe box down beside the garbage bag and picked up the letter. She brushed her fingertips lightly across the signature. Daniel. An elegant sounding name, not blunt and hard like the short form Dan.

She left the basement light on and the door open. Pausing in the front hall, she slipped on her sandals and considered a light jacket. After such a hot day she wouldn't need it. She stuffed the keys in her pocket and turned on the outside light. The door locked behind her but she jiggled the knob just to be sure.

The night was still warm, comfortable after the scorching summer day. The grass beneath her feet felt lush and springy. A thunderstorm two days ago had brought it back from a dried yellowing state.

Katherine reached the road and looked across. The golf course lay shrouded in darkness, but she knew the far end dipped toward the river. The road was empty of traffic. Katherine crossed and walked along the edge of the golf course, following the fence.

The sound of crickets reached her ears and she marveled. She'd never heard such natural sounds in Toronto. She'd forgotten how peaceful it could feel. The crickets seemed to lead her on, along to the end of the golf course.

She turned right, following a new road as it dipped down toward the river. For a short while it followed the golf course then veered off into a sharp decline. Shapeless maples rose in the darkness on both sides of the road, crowding out any possibility of sidewalks. The streetlights were few here, spaced far apart.

Katherine slowed as she followed the decline. She could feel the paper in her hand, hear its soft crackle in the light breeze. The leaves of the maples rustled in response, a secret code she could not understand. She felt suddenly chilly but the breeze was not that cold.

What was she doing here, had she gone completely mad? It was after midnight and here she was walking alone in a badly lit area, too far from any houses. She would never have done this in Toronto. She'd let London's familiarity dull her senses. This was no longer the town of her childhood with the neighborhoods where everyone knew each other and children played confidently in the parks, unmolested by drug dealers or stalkers. London was no longer immune to muggers stalking the streets. She'd been lucky to get this far.

Just turn around and walk back, keeping a

brisk pace, she told herself. No need to panic. She turned. The breeze made the letter in her hand crackle.

She would come tomorrow in the daylight, when it was safe, when it was sane. It made more sense, a smart practical decision. Why did it make her feel so hollow?

She glanced back over her shoulder, down the road that led into a pool of darkness at the bottom. Her eyes adjusted sufficiently to the dark to discern the general shape of the road. The breeze sent her short, mousy brown hair dancing on her forehead. It wouldn't be the same in the daylight, she realized. She wouldn't be able to fully imagine her father, to really feel him. And her mother.

Reluctantly she turned and began to follow the road down. At least she told herself she was reluctant, she told herself that her quickening steps were only the result of the steepness of the decline. Her heart pounded only from the exertion. She clutched the letter only because she didn't want it to fly away in the breeze.

By the time she reached the bottom of the hill she was running. The road forked, branching one way toward the golf club house, a large hulking shape barely visible around the bend. Branching the other way, the road turned down toward the river, toward the footbridge.

She turned left toward the footbridge. The path narrowed further. The trees, with branches hanging low, pressed closer to the road, making her feel almost claustrophobic. The asphalt quickly turned to gravel, continuing to narrow until it was barely two people wide. The vegetation on either side seemed ready to engulf the road at any instant, swallowing her whole as well. The smell of the leaves was sharp in her nostrils, making her feel heady. She realized she'd missed this natural wildness in Toronto, too much concrete and safe, contained parks with manicured lawns and sculpted trees.

Suddenly the footbridge loomed up ahead of her, metal steps leading up to the wooden floor. Rusting girders defined the structure. She remembered the times the city had condemned the bridge and vowed to tear it down. They'd even seal off the entrances but kids would inevitably climb over the barriers and the city was forced to restore the bridge to ensure safety. Once she'd even done it herself, coaxed on by Benny Richmond, his freckled face flushed with excitement above her, his hand reaching out to her. At eleven it had been the thrill of a lifetime, to have Benny Richmond reaching for her hand.

Katherine took a hold of the railing and began to climb.

The metal was cool beneath her hand. All the paint had worn off, leaving a smooth surface. The stairs whined slightly beneath her feet. Another step up and she was on the walkway.

It stretched on forever. The other side was a distant darker smudge on black. Although she couldn't see much of the bridge she felt the suggestion of its form. The beams shot high into the air, arching downward elegantly. Strong cables, invisible in the darkness, tethered the bridge to the land. Katherine didn't need to see them, she remembered watching birds sitting on the cables, swaying in the breeze.

Had her father come onto the bridge from this

side or the park side? Had he lingered at one end, or made his way out to the center? He would walk to the center, she decided. There was no reason for her to think that but she liked the idea.

Again she took a hold of the rail and allowed it to lead her toward the center of the bridge. The water of the Thames, a dark polluted green during the daytime, was now black, an invisible gurgling carpet. The sound of it, an ever present background noise, took center stage, growing louder as she traveled away from the land.

Finally she reached the center and stopped, waiting for the sway of the bridge to finish. She remembered racing with Benny Richmond across the walkway, just to feel the sway. Or they'd jump up and down, then stand still. It was like being able to shake the world.

She laughed out loud, her voice trickling off into the distance. Crickets chirped a response. She loved it here, felt free from everything.

Had he stood at this spot, she wondered. Leaning against the rail, did he smoke a cigarette, tapping off the ash to watch it fall lazily into the water. Daniel.

She imagined her mother coming to meet him. She would have worn a white dress, easier for him to see her. He'd call out to her when she appeared, guiding her with his voice. She'd advance slowly, carefully feeling her way until they stood together. He would have brought her a rose.

Katherine became aware of the tears on her cheeks and she chuckled to herself. What an idiot she was, daydreaming romance for her poor dead mother. Maybe she'd wanted a father more than she realized. It wouldn't make any difference now. For all intents and purposes, she was alone.

As she began to walk back across the bridge a breeze rose up, ruffling her hair. She pushed the bangs out of her eyes and took another step. Her foot missed then slapped on the wood. The bridge was swaying in the breeze, faster than before.

Katherine slowly became aware of her position. The bridge was old, the flooring made up of wooden planks, many probably ready to fall through. She could be plunged into the swift current of the river. What the hell was she thinking?

Get off, she told herself. She grabbed the rail and began sliding her feet forward. Her hair danced around her face, darting in and out of her mouth. The breeze whistled in her ears, making tones, distorting, twisting the crickets and nights sounds into a voice.

Calling her.

Katherine stopped and looked around. The darkness felt thick and heavy. The breeze was cold but sweat trickled down her fleshy sides. Her mouth was dry as she tried to swallow. The breeze lulled, then picked up again.

"Katherine..."

There, she'd heard it. The paper crackled in her hand as she clenched it. The sound made her jump. The bridge swayed a little more beneath her feet.

Someone else was on the bridge.

Never mind it was irrational, or she'd have heard anyone approaching in the stillness, she knew someone was there.

She had to get off the bridge.

She turned around and realized she didn't know which way she was facing. Was it the park in front of her or behind? How many times had she turned? Had she been facing the right way in the first place? Where was the person who was on the bridge with her?

The breeze brushed her arms and she shivered. Goose pimples formed on her arms and beneath her t-shirt. The jeans felt clammy and tight on her legs. She wanted to scream but her throat was so dry she feared it wouldn't make a sound.

"Katherine."

A man's voice spoke from behind her. She gripped the railing until her fingers hurt. She felt colder, much colder than she had any right to feel on this warm evening. She wasn't going to turn around, wasn't going to look. But her head moved of its own volition, turning slowly to the left.

For a moment she expected -- Benny Richmond -- as her mind reached for something to steady her. She could actually see his freckled face and red crewcut before the image faded, turning into...

A man.

He was tall and thin, wearing dark pants and a lighter shirt, the colors hard to discern in the darkness. His skin was white, shining out of the cuffs and neck of his shirt like a beacon. One thin white hand touched the railing. The other brought a cigarette up to his pale lips. The tip flared bright red as he took a drag.

Smoke obscured his face as he released it through his flaring nostrils. When it dissipated she saw he had a proud, aquiline nose and wide blue eyes. A slight smile touched his lips.

"I had no idea you'd come here, Katherine." His voice was a deep rumble, low in his chest.

Katherine shifted a little to face him. How had he snuck up behind her so silently? Why hadn't she smelled his cigarette? She was allergic to smoke and could smell it coming a block away, even outside.

Stall him, keep him talking.

"How do you know my name?" she asked.

"Your mother's told me all about you. She's very proud."

Katherine stiffened. Who was this man to talk about her mother? Anger tinged the edges of her fear, giving her strength.

"Who are you?" she demanded. "What are you doing here, following a woman around in the dark. I could have you arrested!"

He chuckled. "You do have spirit, just like she said. Good to see it." He took another drag on his cigarette, letting the smoke out slowly, watching her with such obvious amusement that her anger swept away her fear.

Then his face slowly lost its humor, becoming more serious. "Don't you know?" he asked. "I thought you'd guessed, that's why you came here."

"Guessed what?" She spoke a little more reticently. His seriousness dispelled her anger, allowing her fear to return.

"I'm your father," he said.

The fear returned in full bloom. Cold sweat trickled down her back. He was a madman, she thought, and she was standing in the middle of a river with him.

"I thought you'd guessed," he repeated. "I did everything she asked. Left you both alone until you'd grown up and moved away. I gave her seven months to straighten everything up, to give you time to get used to her death. I could have taken her in one night but she thought it would be too much of a shock for you."

Katherine stared at him. Was he the one who was mad? She was beginning to wonder. He looked no older than thirty-five. Mousy brown hair ruffled across his forehead in the breeze and he brushed it back with an impatient gesture.

Mousy brown.

Her mother'd had black hair, before it had gone grey. She'd always told Katherine she had her father's hair. Mousy brown.

She stared at him, unable to think of anything to say.

"Daniel, what are you doing?"

Katherine spun at the sound of the voice behind her. A strangled cry gurgled from her throat. She made a grab for the railing as her knees buckled. Her hand missed and she fell to her knees, setting the bridge swaying again.

Her mother stood before her, wearing the cream dress she'd worn in her casket. Her hair hung down to her shoulders and looked almost black. Her face, white even against the light cream of the dress, looked less wrinkled. Katherine's mouth dropped open as tears filled her eyes.

"Oh look what you've done, Daniel," her mother said. "You've upset her."

"We were doing fine, Angela." He sounded hurt. "I thought maybe you'd told her."

"Why would I tell her, for god's sake." Her mother slapped the railing for emphasis in a familiar gesture.

I am crazy, Katherine thought, dazed.

Angela bent down and took Katherine's shoulders. "I know this is a shock, darling, and I'm sorry. What are you doing here?"

"Letter," Katherine managed to croak out of her uncooperative mouth. She glanced at the wadded paper in her hand.

Gently her mother extracted the paper from her fingers. As she smoothed it out, Katherine wondered at the coldness of her touch.

Angela stood after she read the letter, folding it carefully in half. "Oh dear," she said to Daniel. "She found the letter you sent me last September."

"I told you it wasn't my fault."

Angela bent again and helped Katherine to her feet. Up close she looked younger than she had a right to, but her breath smelled foul.

"You think you're crazy, right, Katherine?" Her mother smiled as a flicker of emotion crossed Katherine's face.

"I always knew what you were thinking. But you're not crazy, although you'll probably wish you were." Her voice paused, her expression hesitant. "You see, your father and I are... undead."

The river roared in Katherine's ears. She closed her eyes to wash away the vision before her.

"I've been this way since I died. When I first met your father thirty-five years ago, he was... that way too. When I found out I was pregnant with you I made him swear not to take me until you'd grown up and were on your own."

Katherine opened her eyes to look into her mother's white face. She looked almost as young as when Katherine was a child.

"You look younger," she whispered.

Angela smiled slightly, parting her lips to expose a neat row of sharp looking teeth. "Your father first bit me when I was thirty. Now that I'm an undead, my body is returning to the original state it was in when I was first bitten." Her smile widened. "I'll stay young."

Katherine shook her head. This was too much for her to deal with. She had to be dreaming. She was probably still in the basement, propped up in the kitchen chair beside the garbage bag. When she woke up, she'd have an awful kink in her neck.

The breeze stirred the water beneath the bridge, making it gurgle. Katherine became aware of Daniel standing close beside her. She started. She hadn't heard him move.

"Angela has told me so much about you," he said. A white hand reached up to touch her hair. She shied away.

"I wish I could have seen you grow up but your mother insisted otherwise. She was right of course, but I am glad you've come here to join us."

Katherine's eyes widen. Join them? She took a step back and felt the rail press against her buttocks. The wood beneath her feet creaked.

A shadow passed over her mother's face. "Daniel?"

"Of course, it's natural for you to want to be with your parents. I always believed that was the way it should have been all along." Daniel stepped closer. His face glowed in the darkness, his blue eyes darkening. Behind his pale lips, Katherine saw his tongue lick over two long, pointed incisors.

"Daniel, no!" Angela grabbed his arm and pulled. She managed only to halt him. "This wasn't part of our agreement."

"What's the difference? We can all be together," he said. He looked back at Katherine. "Besides, I haven't fed tonight."

He took another step. With a cry, Angela pounced.

The bridge swayed as they struggled. Holding onto the rail, Katherine backed away. They fought like animals, snarling and snapping. Daniel sank his teeth into Angela's shoulders. Her shriek echoed off the treetops.

Katherine turned and ran. The bridge pitched beneath her feet. Several times she stumbled, falling against the railing, bruising her hip. The snarls of the fight followed her.

Almost to the end of the bridge she stumbled again, landing on her knees. She grabbed for the rail. There was a groan of metal and a piece snapped off in her hand. She landed on her chest, the air pushed out of her, her face over the edge.

The stench of the river filled her nostrils as she gasped for air. Slowly she crawled away from the edge, still clutching the three foot piece of metal railing.

"No!"

Her mother's cry reached her. Katherine looked. Her mother had fallen to her knees, hands scratching uselessly against Daniel's back as he bent over her.

He's killing her, Katherine thought, and then he'll come for me.

She struggled to her feet, trying to recall the vampire lore she knew. Mostly it was from the old Hammer films. Stake through the heart, garlic, sunlight, something about running water. It was all she could remember.

She didn't have a stake, but she did have the railing.

The broken tip was jagged, not exactly a point. Flaking paint scratched her hand as she gripped it, sweat making it slip. The edges dug into her fingers. Her heart pounded in her chest as if she'd run up a flight of stairs too fast. There was only one chance.

Her mother cried out again, weakly. Her hands fluttered slightly. Daniel growled low.

Raising the rail like a javelin, Katherine began to run. The bridge swayed, keeping pace. The darkened forms drew closer, larger. She aimed for the left side of Daniel's back.

He seemed to sense her, straightening. To Katherine he moved in slow motion, his strong back slowly pulling itself erect. She tightened her grip on the rail. Aimed. Thrust.

He shrieked as the rail pierced his back. Droplets of blood splashed back into Katherine's face. She threw all her weight behind the rail, driving it farther. Daniel fell forward, knocking her mother over. Katherine stumbled and landed on his legs. Her left foot slipped over the edge of the walkway. She felt coolness reflected from the water below.

She scrambled off him, clinging to the wooden planks. The bridge swayed, creaking as if to protest all this activity. Katherine reached forward and touched the hem of her mother's dress.

"Momma?"

Angela stirred. She tried to sit up, but her arms trembled violently. "Katherine, help me," she whispered.

Katherine wrapped her arms around her mother and lifted her away, carrying her a few feet. She weighed no more than a bundle of sticks, Katherine thought in dismay.

When released, Angela could not support herself and sank down to the wooden floor. Her skin was no longer white but almost translucent. Her neck and shoulder were torn open, revealing bloodless muscle and scratched bone.

Looking past her, Katherine saw Daniel had not moved. He lay face down, the rail protruding from his back like a mast.

"I'll be right back," she said.

Angela nodded weakly.

Katherine crept forward and turned Daniel over. His face was frozen in an expression of shock, blood staining his mouth like lipstick. The tip of the rail protruded through the front of his shirt almost bashfully.

She returned to her mother and knelt. "He's dead, momma."

Angela raised her hand and tried to touch Katherine's face. "I'm so sorry. I didn't want to hurt you."

Katherine shook her head. "No, I'm the one who's sorry. I shouldn't have found that letter." Her throat dried up, making it difficult to talk.

"I wanted to keep everything. I didn't want you to go."

Angela smiled. "I didn't want to leave either. Maybe we were both wrong."

Katherine took her mother's hand, so cold, skin almost clear, and held it to her tear stained cheek.

Neither said anything more. They sat until morning, until the sky began to lighten and the birds began to sing. Angela struggled, trying to pull herself to her feet but she was too weak. Desperately she clutched at Katherine's ankles. The wounds in her neck and shoulder looked blanched, bits of skin flapping in the breeze.

"Help," Angela pleaded. Her voice strained but still didn't get above a whisper.

Katherine knelt down. She wanted to take hold of her mother, comfort her. If she ran quickly she could carry her mother back to the house before the sun was over the horizon. She leaned forward.

"Katherine," her mother whispered.

One of her teeth flashed white in the

approaching brightness. Katherine pulled back, startled. She stared at Angela's face. It was her mother's face but the eyes were too dark, too intense, too desperate. Her mother had never looked like that, even in the worst times. Your dignity is all you have, she'd say.

Said.

Mother is dead, Katherine thought. For the first time in three months the thought did not make her want to cry. A calm settled over her. Mother was dead and Katherine had been lucky, so very lucky to have had her. But she was gone now. This creature before her was only a bad copy, a husk.

"I'll stay with you until it's done," Katherine said. She owed her mother, her mother's memory that.

Feeling Angela scrape weakly at her hand, Katherine turned her face to welcome the sun.

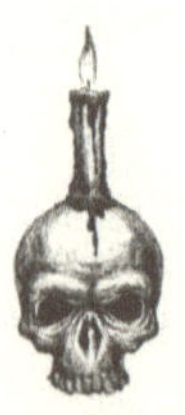

SOUL HUNGRY

When Wendy opened her eyes, the bathroom was covered in blood. It splashed the tiles in long streaks. Brown puddles congealed on the linoleum. Globs splattered the mirror as if thrown from a paint brush. Clots of blood squished in her hair. Slowly, she sat up. Her body ached, the muscles spasming. Leaning on the toilet, she peeled her underwear off. The blood looked almost black. She threw her underwear at the sink. It hit the porcelain with a sickly smack. The sound made her stomach churn but she was too spent to vomit. Thank god Chuck wouldn't see this mess.

Fatigue drowned all other emotions. The last few weeks she had gone through them all; anger, fear, horror, relief. All she had left was fatigue.

Slowly she climbed into the tub and turned the shower on. As the water streamed down, she turned her face to it. Rivulets sped down her back. The water ran red and soon she could comb her fingers through her hair without feeling the clumps. The ache in her muscles faded to a dull throb and strength began to return. She would have to take a muscle relaxant to ease them completely. She scrubbed soap into her skin, scraping over and over. Her flesh turned pink then red. Finally she stopped and lifted her face to the water to rinse. She stepped out of the tub, avoiding the worst puddles. The blood had dried to rusty brown flakes with jagged edges like teeth.

Wendy closed the bathroom door behind her and sagged against it. Sunlight slanted in through the bedroom windows, showing the tousled bed sheets. It had to be mid morning and she had a doctor's appointment at eleven. Wendy forced her trembling legs to carry her to the dresser and pulled out clothing. Her hand paused in the drawer. Should she clean up the bathroom? No, she'd leave it. With Chuck gone, there was no rush. She'd clean it later.

By ten thirty she was on the road. She would make the appointment. Her palms were slick on the leather steering wheel.

Cervical cancer, the doctor had told her. Had it only been six weeks ago? Time distorted in her mind. Surely it had been months or hadn't the doctor just told her yesterday? She couldn't remember anymore. How fragile was her life that it had disintegrated in that short time? First the abnormal pap test, then the colposcopy with the doctor peering at her cervix through a microscope. She'd felt vaguely ridiculous with her legs in the stirrups, spread wide to the world. But when the doctor pointed to the monitor, she knew it wasn't funny.

And it wasn't cervical cancer.

Remembering the image in the television monitor, Wendy shuddered. Her hands tightened on the wheel. Her breathing quickened.

A small black center surrounded by a perfect red circle that swirled like a vortex, expanding even as she watched. Her breath caught in her throat. That was inside her.

Precancerous, the doctor said. But she knew it was something else, could feel it shifting inside her like a live thing. A hunger inside her. A red, swirling hunger, more terrifying than any cancer cell.

A cone biopsy was all she needed, the doctor had assured her. As she listened, the blood rushed in her ears like an ocean roar. Her heart thudded in her chest. A simple operation to remove the precancerous section, that was as far as it would go. Probably she wouldn't need a hysterectomy. That had been two weeks ago. Then they'd called her back: come in today.

The bleeding had started after the biopsy but she hadn't mentioned it to her doctor. He would have hospitalized her at once and she knew that would kill her. Somehow the hunger would blame her and strike her down. She felt tired and sore after the bleeding but not weaker. It was punishing her, trying to make her understand, trying to make her feed it.

Her attempts to talk to Chuck had run smack into his indifference. She'd tried not to notice, tried to ignore his remarks the way she tried to ignore his hand grabbing her arm or his drunken fumbles in the night. He was under a lot of stress. It was difficult to be out of work while your wife continued to rise in her career. She tried to understand.

But then the cancer came and he'd looked at her like she was some kind of monster, some diseased thing. After the colposcopy, she'd come home tired and sore from a biopsy they'd taken. He'd seemed sympathetic as he tucked her into bed, even kissed her forehead as she closed her eyes.

His hot breath woke her. Dusk dimmed the room to shades of grey. He'd pulled the cover off her and pushed her nightgown to her waist.

His knees parted her legs. His hand stroked her belly.

"Don't, Chuck," she moaned. "They said not for twenty-four hours."

"They don't know anything, baby." His voice was low, insistent. "I know what you need."

She struggled, but he pinned her down and soon he slid inside. He began to pump. The dull ache turned to piercing pain. With every pound she felt a spike in her belly. Her whimpers of pain mingled with his moans. Then, without her consent, she felt a familiar flutter of pleasure. Her cries got louder but his moans matched hers. He was now sliding easily, slipping in and out. She hardly felt it. Her breath caught as he shuddered and stopped. His own grunt ended in a gurgle.

He landed on her, slick with sweat. She stroked his hair. It was soaked.

"Quite the workout," she muttered. He didn't respond. She shook his shoulder. "Chuck?"

Her fingers fumbled for the lamp on the night stand.

His face looked wizened, his features sinking

in on themselves even as she watched. With a shriek, she pushed him off. He felt weightless as a corn husk and slid off the edge of the bed. From the waist down she was all blood. She screamed. He had ruptured something in her! Bile burned her throat. Her heart hammered. But as she touched the congealing pool between her legs, she realized it wasn't hers. The swirl of red with a black center. The hunger. Now satisfied.

Getting rid of Chuck had been easier than she'd expected. Even as she cleaned up the bedroom, his form shrank more. His skin flaked. She spread out an old sheet and rolled him into it. While she wondered how and where she would take him, he dissolved.

She should feel sorry. Sorry for the times he stole money from her purse. Sorry when he didn't come home until after midnight with some lame excuse about the car. Sorry she'd pretended not to smell the perfume on his shirt.

Nobody questioned her story of him leaving her. Somehow that seemed worse but she forgot it in the rush of good health that followed. After the cone biopsy, she recovered remarkably fast. Her doctor complimented her recuperative powers.

But now her blood coated the bathroom. Looking in the rearview mirror, she could see that her face was pale, her eyes bloodshot. Her stomach tightened. What was she going to do?

"I'm a little tired today," she told the doctor.

He nodded absently. "I know you're anxious to hear the results of the cone biopsy. I'm sorry to say that the precancerous cells look like they go farther than I expected. We could try another cone biopsy but I think we'll just get the same result. I recommend a hysterectomy."

Wendy's abdomen churned. Maybe that was the answer. Maybe they could cut it all out, rid her of it.

"When?" she asked.

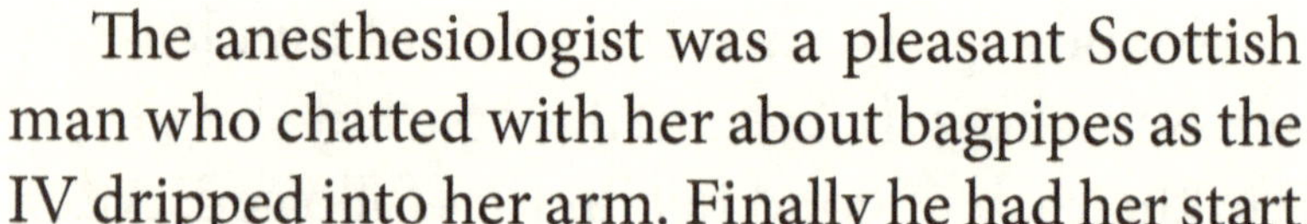

The anesthesiologist was a pleasant Scottish man who chatted with her about bagpipes as the IV dripped into her arm. Finally he had her start counting down from a hundred. She made it to ninety-four.

When she woke, her body felt like a huge bruise, originating at her abdomen. A murmuring nurse came in to give her a shot. Words like "a slight complication" and "several days" rolled over her mind, barely registering. All she noticed was the ceiling of the room. White plaster swirled in a circular pattern, getting closer and tighter toward the center. She watched the swirls rotate as her eyelids shut. Before they closed completely, the ceiling turned red.

The next time she woke, the doctor stood reading her chart. He looked up as she opened her eyes. He hooked the chart back onto the foot of her bed and stepped forward.

"I'm glad you're awake, Wendy, I wanted to tell you as soon as you woke."

She struggled to focus on him. "Tell me what?"

He set the chart down and took her hand.

"We had some problems. I'm afraid we had

to take your ovaries as well and we had to cut more of the vagina that I wanted to. We then had to sew you up and there isn't much left. I'm so sorry."

His expression was pensive, unsure of her reaction, but she smiled. Relief flooded her, giving her some feeble strength. They'd done it, they'd cut it out and not only that, they'd sealed the opening. It couldn't come back.

"I understand," she whispered and closed her eyes as the doctor stepped away.

They kept her in the hospital more than a week to make sure she healed properly. Several times they tried to get her to see a therapist but she would have none of it. She didn't need to talk to anyone. Who would believe what she had to say, that she was happy to be rid of the red, swirling hunger that had killed Chuck? Now she didn't have to worry about more blood or the emptiness that filled her with desire until she thought she would scream. Now it was gone and she could live again. Relief washed away the last of her fear.

When they released her, she took a cab home. She didn't want to share this with anyone. Her mother would only fuss and annoy her, besides, she felt strong and healthy. Finally, she was healthy.

She paid the driver, entered her apartment building and took the elevator to her floor. She lived at the far end of the hall and the walk from the elevator wore her out. Not as strong as she'd thought. But even the weakness had a healthy feel to it. She chuckled to herself. It was a normal tired.

Her mother had piled her mail on the dining room table, sorting it into bills, letters and miscellaneous. She'd even stacked the junk mail in a neat pile. Typical Mom.

She'd look at it later. Right now she wanted a nap. She shrugged off her jacket and tossed it on the couch. Kicking off her shoes, she walked to the bedroom. Without turning on the light, she groped to the bed and fell in.

Hours later, a warmth on her body woke her. It spread across her stomach and chest like a large questing hand. It smothered her throat and nose. She'd fallen asleep in her clothes, no wonder she was so hot. She tried to turn over. Pain pierced her stomach.

Wendy clutched the sheets, gasping. They were soaked. Her heart pounded. It shook her body, forcing her to lie back. Her hands released the sheets and touched her stomach. It was wet. Oh god, it was wet.

She whimpered. Sweat trickled down her face. Her hands reached down, touched her stomach, her thighs...

A wide, open cavity.

She screamed. Her heart thudded, spurting thick blood over her hands. But even as it flowed, it sucked back into her. Inside her belly.

She reached for the night table, fumbling for the light. She got it but it fell to the floor, casting crazy shadows on the ceiling and walls.

Her legs were covered in blood. She couldn't move them, couldn't feel them. As she watched, her thighs flattened and a gush of blood welled in the cavity of her abdomen. Then it settled like a tide, rising, falling. Pain shuddered up her spine.

She almost passed out but was denied even that relief. Her mind hung on even as she willed it to surrender. Hot pain stabbed her torso, pounded in her temples.

She'd been wrong. She had thought they could cut it out but that wasn't what they had done. That red swirling mass had been a hunger; a pure, unforgiving compulsion. Instead of cutting it out, they had sealed it in. She had to feed it or it would feed itself, the way it had with Chuck. The way it was now.

Blood gurgled in her lungs. She watched her intestines shudder and shiver. Too late now, even if she had the strength to reach for the phone. Her legs were gone. She watched them wither. The bones of her knees stuck out like marbles, her skin stretched thin and transparent. Then her legs deflated and her veins flattened on the bed sheet.

Wendy closed her eyes. Another spike of pain shot up to her head. Her jaw clamped down, severing the tip of her tongue. Her lungs burned now. Her heart pounded in panic as if it could escape her rib cage. But there was no escape.

The hunger scorched her nerves. Pain trailed in its wake. Shrinking muscles bent her hands into claws. The skin along her arms peeled back. Her fingers snapped as she grabbed at the bed sheet. Her lungs collapsed. She opened her mouth to shriek but blood filled her throat. Her eyelids fluttered open, dissolved into her forehead. The muscles in her face shriveled. She stared at the ceiling, screaming in her mind, as the hunger devoured her.

ABOUT THE AUTHOR

REBECCA M. SENESE weaves words of horror, mystery, contemporary fantasy, and science fiction in Toronto, Canada. She is the author of the contemporary fantasy series, the Noel Kringle Chronicles featuring the son of Santa Claus working as a private detective in Toronto. She garnered an Honorable Mention in "The Year's Best Science Fiction" and has been nominated for numerous Aurora Awards. Her work has appeared in numerous Holiday Hijinks anthologies including *Whimsical Winter Wonderland*, *Happy Holiday Historicals*, *Tidbits & Tinsel Tales*, *Haunted Holidays*, *Mistletoe Merriment*, *Crazy Christmas Capers*, and *Toy Trucks and Teddy Bears*. She has also appeared in *Home for the Howlidays*, *Pulphouse Fiction Magazine*, *Unmasked: Tales of Risk and Revelation*, the *Obsessions Anthology*, *Fiction River: Superpowers*, *Fiction River: Visions of the Apocalypse*, *Fiction River: Sparks*, *Fiction River: Recycled Pulp*, *Tesseracts 16: Parnassus Unbound*, *Tesseracts 15: A Case of Quite Curious Tales*, *Ride the Moon*, *Hungar Magazine*, *On Spec*, *TransVersions*, and *Storyteller*, amongst others.

FIND ME ONLINE

RebeccaSenese.com

RebeccaSeneseBooks.com